# Ollie's Easter Eggs

## Olivier Dunrea

HOUGHTON MIFFLIN HARCOURT
Boston   New York

**To access the read-along audio file, visit**
**WWW.HMHBOOKS.COM/FREEDOWNLOADS**
**ACCESS CODE: MYEGG**

| AGES | GRADES | GUIDED READING LEVEL | READING RECOVERY LEVEL | LEXILE® LEVEL |
|------|--------|----------------------|------------------------|---------------|
| 4-6 | 1 | F | 9-10 | 320L |

www.hmhco.com

The text of this book is set in MShannon.
The illustrations are pen-and-ink and gouache on 140-pound d'Arches coldpress
watercolor paper.

The library of Congress Cataloging-in-Publication Data is on file.

ISBN: 978-0-544-80911-6 paperback
ISBN: 978-0-544-80972-7 paper-over-board

Manufactured in China
SCP 10 9 8 7 6 5 4 3 2 1

4500618896

*To Anita and Lin—*
*who shared many Easter*
*egg hunts with me*

This is Gossie and Gertie.
They are gathering eggs.

This is BooBoo and Peedie.
They are gathering eggs, too.

This is Ollie.

He is hopping.

Gossie dyes her egg
bright red.

Gertie dyes her egg
bright blue.

BooBoo dyes her egg
bright purple.

Peedie dyes his egg
bright yellow.

Ollie stares at the
brightly colored eggs.

"I want eggs!" he shouts.

Gossie hides her egg
in the green grass.

"My egg," whispers Ollie.
He rolls the red egg out
of sight.

Gertie hides her egg
in the yellow straw.

"My egg," whispers Ollie.
He rolls the blue egg out
of sight.

BooBoo hides her egg
in the red tulips.

"My egg," whispers Ollie.
He rolls the purple egg out
of sight.

Peedie hides his egg
under the green turtle.

"My egg," whispers Ollie.
He rolls the yellow egg out
of sight.

Ollie hides all the eggs
under his blanket.

Gossie and Gertie hunt
for the Easter eggs.
They look in the tulips.

They look under the turtle.

BooBoo and Peedie hunt
for the Easter eggs.
They look in the grass.

They look in the straw.

Gossie and Gertie
scoot past Ollie.

Searching. Hunting.

BooBoo and Peedie
scurry past Ollie.

Hunting. Searching.

"Look!" Ollie says. Four small
goslings stop and stare.
"Easter eggs!" shouts Ollie.